For Dylan Parker, the newest little star, shining bright

SIMON & SCHUSTER BOOKS FOR YOUNG READERS
An imprint of Simon & Schuster Children's Publishing Division
1230 Avenue of the Americas, New York, New York 10020
Copyright © 2018 by Raúl Colón
SIMON & SCHUSTER BOOKS FOR YOUNG READERS is a trademark of Simon & Schuster, Inc.
For information about special discounts for bulk purchases, please contact Simon & Schuster Special Sales
at 1-866-506-1949 or business@simonandschuster.com.
The Simon & Schuster Speakers Bureau can bring authors to your live event.
For more information or to book an event, contact the Simon & Schuster Speakers Bureau
at 1-866-248-3049 or visit our website at www.simonspeakers.com.
Book design by Laurent Linn
The text for this book was set in Casablanca.
The illustrations for this book are rendered in watercolors, Prismacolor pencils, and lithograph pencils on Arches paper.
Manufactured in China · 0618 SCP · First Edition
2 4 6 8 10 9 7 5 3 1
Library of Congress Cataloging-in-Publication Data
Names: Colón, Raúl, author, illustrator.
Title: Imagine! / Raúl Colón.
Description: First edition. | New York : Simon & Schuster Books for Young Readers, [2018] | "A Paula Wiseman Book." |
Summary: "When a boy visits an art museum and one of the paintings comes to life, he has an afternoon of adventure and discovery
[that] changes how he sees the world ever after"—Provided by publisher.
Identifiers: LCCN 2017000920| ISBN 9781481462730 (hardcover) | ISBN 9781481462747 (eBook)
Subjects: | CYAC: Perception—Fiction. | Imagination—Fiction. | Art museums—Fiction. | Museums—Fiction. | Stories without words.
Classification: LCC PZ7.C716365 Im 2017 | DDC [E]—dc23
LC record available at https://lccn.loc.gov/2017000920

IMAGINE!

RAÚL COLÓN

A Paula Wiseman Book

SIMON & SCHUSTER BOOKS FOR YOUNG READERS

New York London Toronto Sydney New Delhi

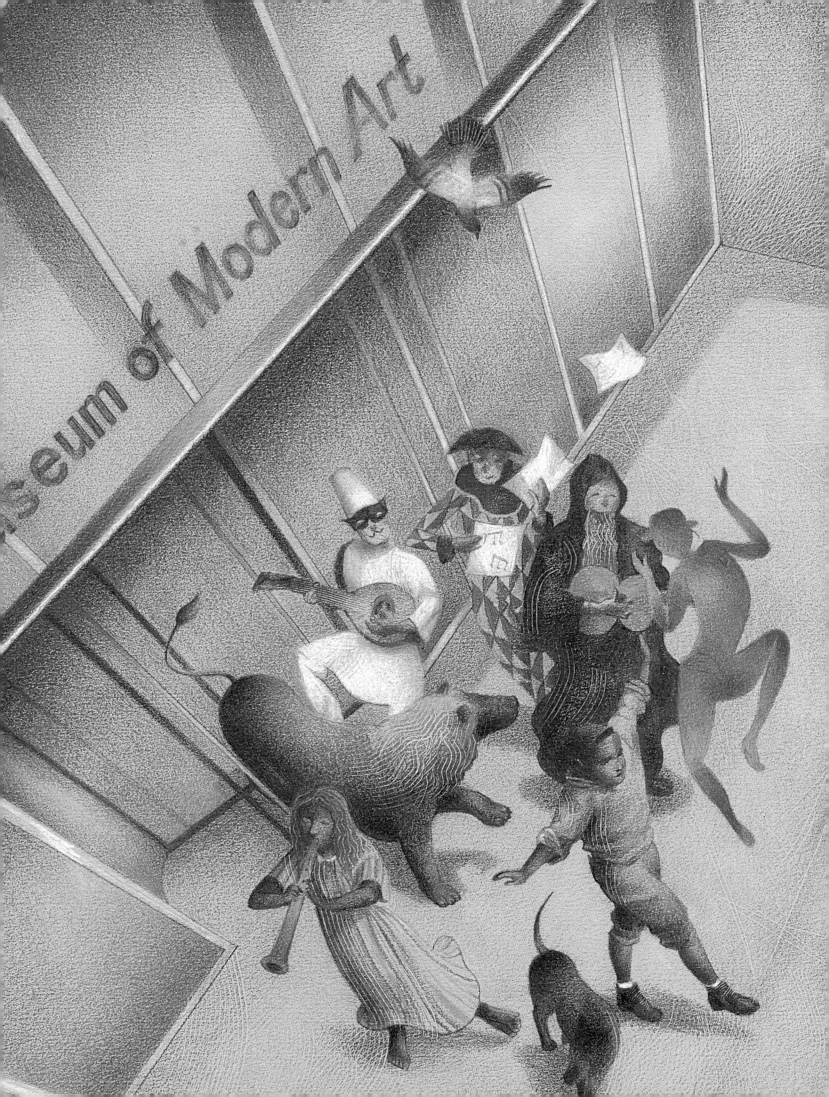

The Museum of Mode

AUTHOR'S NOTE

Even though I lived in New York City, the only museum I had visited was the American Museum of Natural History, during a school excursion. My hardworking parents were taking care of many important issues to help keep the family above water and my fragile health in check. However, every Sunday I would look forward to my dad's trip to the local candy store to buy his newspapers, magazines, and paperbacks. He always brought my sister and me along. We were allowed to buy our own comic books and magazines: anything from *Archie* to *Spider-Man*, or DC Comics's *Men of War*. This is how I was introduced to Steve Ditko's and Joe Kubert's art, along with many other artists. My days with anything artistic were usually spent at home with books and comics and notebooks in my hand. I drew and drew. I would copy what I was seeing on the printed page, including paintings like Van Gogh's.

As an adult, on my first visit to an art museum, *Starry Night* was right there, facing me. I had never seen it like this. Even though I was an adult, I reacted like a child. The emotions I felt were overwhelming. There are many paintings that have inspired me over the years, but I have included Pablo Picasso's *Three Musicians*, Henri Rousseau's *The Sleeping Gypsy*, and Henri Matisse's *Icarus* in this book because I felt they represented what would work best for this particular story. They all have interesting characters, movement, color, and a sense of whimsy that would go well with the adventure the boy is about to enjoy. *Starry Night* by Vincent Van Gogh was considered, but I couldn't quite fit it into this story. I hope all readers can visit the Museum of Modern Art in New York one day and see this beautiful painting in person.

I believe that visiting the art museum and experiencing all the other countless works of art I knew only through reproductions became one of the most rewarding experiences in my development as an illustrator. My mind was freed and I felt compelled and confident to express what was inside me and to create what wasn't. Seeing the works of great artists then and now gives me inspiration and stimulates my imagination.

I wonder what would it have meant for me if I actually had seen all these wonders when I was much younger? What if I would have been there on my own? What an adventure that would have been.

Imagine! addresses that idea. A boy decides to take that eventful journey toward the incredible land of creation and suddenly his brain is on fire, trapped in his own critical thinking and pure inspiration that leads him through a fantasy tour with a few of the iconic characters he's seen on the museum walls, eventually creating his own inspired piece on another wall.

I can only hope that young readers (and older ones too) experience these visuals and want to visit the nearest museum to free their own minds and explore their thoughts—away from the gadgets and the screens that sometimes are designed to "think" for us.

Maybe their minds will explode and fireworks will go off and floodgates will open, creating sparks that lead them to their own revelations like mine did.

Imagine that!